Annie
Finds Sandy

Written by Fran Manushkin
Illustrated by George Wildman
Based on characters drawn by Leonard Starr

Random House

Copyright © 1982 Tribune Company Syndicate, Inc. All rights reserved under International and Pan-American Copyright Conventions. Published in the United States by Random House, Inc., New York, and simultaneously in Canada by Random House of Canada Limited, Toronto. Library of Congress Catalog Card Number: 81-52851 ISBN: 0-394-85208-7 Manufactured in the United States of America   3 4 5 6 7 8 9 0

Annie was a little girl with red hair. She lived in Miss Hannigan's orphanage with six other girls.

She hated it—because Miss
Hannigan was mean to everybody.

So one day Annie decided to run away.

She packed everything she owned: her extra underwear, her sweater, and her bottle-cap collection.

Then Annie hugged her friends good-bye and hid in a laundry basket.

When Mr. Bundles came for the laundry,
he loaded Annie right onto his truck.

Mr. Bundles headed straight to his shop and
started tossing the baskets into a dark basement.

"Leapin' lizards!" Annie yelled. "I'm getting out of here!" And she jumped up and ran away as fast as she could.

"I'm free!" Annie shouted. "Hurray!" She started walking down the busy, crowded street, and some raggedy boys ran right past her. They were chasing a scruffy old dog.

"Yelp!" cried the dog again and again.
"Poor dog," said Annie. "They tied cans to your tail."

Annie ran over to the boys.
"Stop that!" she shouted.
"Try and make me," sneered the biggest boy, Spike.
"All right," Annie said, and she kicked him—<u>hard</u>!

"OUCH!" Spike shouted. He tried to hit Annie back, but she kicked him again.

"YIKES!" Spike yelled. "This girl's dangerous!" And he ran away with the rest of his gang.

Annie bent down and untied the cans from the dog's tail. "Gee, they really hurt you," she said softly. "But now you're going to be okay."

"Listen," Annie told him, "I can't give you a home. I don't even have one myself."

But the dog just wouldn't go away. "I guess I'll have to outrun you," said Annie. And she raced down the block. The dog looked sad. He didn't even try to catch up to her.

The old dog lay his head in Annie's lap. "I'll sing you a little song," she said. The dog liked it so much that he cheered up. He even wagged his tail.

"Good boy." Annie smiled and patted him. "Now, I've got to find my real family. So, good-bye!" Annie walked away, but the old dog trotted along behind her.